THE CLASH
OF THE WITHERS

THE CLASH
OF THE WITHERS
AN UNOFFICIAL MINECRAFTERS TIME TRAVEL ADVENTURE
BOOK ONE

Winter Morgan

Sky Pony Press
New York

Copyright © 2018 by Hollan Publishing, Inc.

Minecraft® is a registered trademark of Notch Development AB.

The Minecraft game is copyright © Mojang AB.

Sky Pony Press books may be purchased in bulk at special discounts for sales promotion, corporate gifts, fund-raising, or educational purposes. Special editions can also be created to specifications. For details, contact the Special Sales Department, Sky Pony Press, 307 West 36th Street, 11th Floor, New York, NY 10018 or info@skyhorsepublishing.com.

Sky Pony® is a registered trademark of Skyhorse Publishing, Inc.®, a Delaware corporation.

Minecraft® is a registered trademark of Notch Development AB.
The Minecraft game is copyright © Mojang AB.

Visit our website at www.skyponypress.com.

10 9 8 7 6 5 4 3 2 1

Library of Congress Cataloging-in-Publication Data is available on file.

Cover design by Brian Peterson
Cover photo by Megan Miller

Print ISBN: 978-1-5107-3735-8
Ebook ISBN: 978-1-5107-3740-2

Printed in the United States of America

TABLE OF CONTENTS

THE CLASH
OF THE WITHERS

1

PRACTICAL JOKES

"**D**o you have the pickaxe?" asked Brett.

Poppy nodded with a giggle. "Are we really going to dig the hole?"

"Of coursc," Brett smiled.

"I hope Joe doesn't get mad when he falls down it," said Poppy.

"He's going to laugh. I promise you," Brett reassured her. "Remember what happened last week?"

Brett and Poppy had a reputation for pranking people in Meadow Mews. Just last week, they completed one of their ultimate pranks. They had booby-trapped their friend Nancy's house. When she walked through the door, a bunch of cookies fell on her head.

"Is the hole deep enough?" Brett asked. This prank on Joe was going to be the biggest prank they had ever pulled on anyone, he thought.

"No." Poppy giggled. "We have to make it deep enough that only his head is seen from the top."

"Great idea." Brett banged his pickaxe deep into the blocky ground and warned Poppy, "We don't have that much time. Joe is going to be here soon."

"Have you met Joe before?" questioned Poppy.

"No, but he's the new apprentice. He's going to help me on the farm. He just moved here from the cold biome. After we complete this farm, I'm going to stay with him in the cold biome and teach them how to build a farm on ice," said Brett.

"Wow, I can't wait for you guys to build a bigger farm in Meadow Mews," Poppy said, and she rattled off a list of ways they could improve the farm.

"I agree," said Brett. "The farm needs a lot of work. I have a big job ahead of me. We have to build a new irrigation system. It's not going to be easy, but I think when it's done, the town of Meadow Mews will have a big enough farm to sustain it for a while."

Poppy was a builder. People from around the Overworld invited her to build skyscrapers. She was an expert at crafting large office buildings. She once built one that went so high up into the sky that Brett thought it touched the clouds. She had been asked to work on a project in the desert, and she had to leave that afternoon. She reminded Brett, "This is my last day before I go to the desert. So I want to see this prank work before I go. I won't be able to have any fun when I leave. I can't prank on a construction site because it's too dangerous."

"I get it," Brett said as sweat formed on his forehead. They had been digging for a while, and he was tired. He hoped he had enough energy left to construct the farm.

Poppy dug another block out of the hole and then hopped in. "Do you see my head?"

"Yes." He laughed. "Just the top."

"This is going to be a great introduction," Poppy said as she climbed out of the hole.

Poppy fixed her purple pigtails and adjusted her pink shirt. "Okay, now we just have to wait for Joe."

"He should be here soon," Brett said.

"I hope so," said Poppy. "I really don't want to miss this."

"There's also an opening ceremony for the new farm. Can you stay for that?" Brett asked.

Poppy wasn't sure. She knew she had to be in the desert by morning, and she didn't like to travel when it was dark because she feared being attacked by hostile mobs. "If I TP to the new job, I can stay for the ceremony."

"Then you should. I want you there. This is my big project, and you're my best friend." As Brett spoke, he saw a man with blue hair dressed in a black leather jacket walk toward them. "I think that's Joe," said Brett.

2

NEW FRIEND

As Joe walked toward them, Poppy tried to control her giggling. "I am going to lead him to the hole."

"We can't pull a prank on him the minute we see him," said Brett. "We have to introduce ourselves. We want to make a good impression."

"I know, but I can't wait to see his face when he falls down the hole. It will be priceless."

Joe walked over to them. "Hi"—he put his hand out to shake—"are you Brett?"

"Yes," Brett said. "And this is my friend Poppy."

"It's great to meet you guys. I've actually heard of you, Poppy. I saw your building in my hometown."

"Where's that?" she asked.

"Farmer's Bay," he responded.

"Oh, that's where I built a skyscraper by the shore. I loved it there."

"I also visited the castle you have outside of the village in Meadow Mews. You are very talented," Joe remarked.

"Thanks," Poppy grinned.

Joe said, "I also was warned that when you guys get together, you like to play pranks on people. I hope you weren't planning to play any on me." Joe raised an eyebrow as he scanned the area, as if he were searching for any possible items they could use to prank him.

"We'd never do anything like that," Poppy replied with a smirk.

"From your expression, I have a feeling you might not be telling the truth," said Joe.

Brett didn't respond to Joe's comment. "We have the opening ceremony happening soon, and I want to show you around the farm before we begin." Brett pointed to a large stretch of land. "We can use all of that land."

"Wow," Joe said as he walked around the grassy patch. "This is going to be the biggest farm I've ever worked on. I am so thankful you asked me to be an apprentice on this farm. I know I'm going to learn a lot while I'm here."

"Do you have a place to stay?" asked Brett.

"Not yet," Joe replied.

"You can stay in my house," Poppy offered. "I will be away building a skyscraper in the desert."

"Thank you," said Joe. "I was looking for a place to stay."

"And I promise that I didn't booby-trap it and you

won't be pranked while you're staying there. You just have to take care of my ocelot, Sam, when I'm gone."

"I love ocelots," said Joe. "I'll take care of Sam."

"I have to show you around the farm," Brett reminded him.

Crowds of people were walking toward the farm, and the mayor of Meadow Mews hurried in their direction.

Mayor Allens rushed over. "Are you guys ready? We have to start the ceremony."

"Yes," Brett said as he spotted Joe walking near the hole. He signaled to Poppy to move Joe away from the hole. He didn't want his apprentice falling in, because there was an audience.

Brett turned around and saw Joe was even closer to the hole. "Joe," he hollered.

Joe stopped. "Is everything okay?"

"Yes," said Brett, "I just need you here to stand beside me as I discuss the farm."

Joe stopped in front of the hole. "There's a large hole in the ground. We have to fill that in, or someone might get hurt."

"Thanks for letting us know. We will fix it," said Poppy.

As the crowds grew, Poppy placed blocks in the hole, but the mayor called her over, and she never got to cover it.

"Poppy will be representing our town as she leaves to construct her sixth skyscraper." The town applauded. The mayor continued, "When she returns home, Poppy will build a large skyscraper in our town."

There were more cheers. Poppy blushed. She was never comfortable getting a lot of attention.

The mayor announced the opening of the farm and discussed how the town would benefit from the wheat and other crops that would grow on the farm. Brett gave a lecture on the importance of farming and irrigation. When he was done, they feasted on cookies and cake.

The sun was beginning to set, and the group disbanded. While Poppy, Brett, and Joe walked back to their homes, Joe asked, "You guys wanted me to trip and fall down that hole, didn't you?"

Poppy and Brett looked at each other. They started to laugh. They couldn't lie. "Yeah," said Brett.

"Sorry," Poppy explained. "We thought it would be funny."

"I'm going to stay one step ahead of you," said Joe.

"Good luck," said Poppy.

"Watch out!" Brett cried as a barrage of arrows flew in their direction. They were under attack.

3
IN THE DARKNESS

The armed skeletons surrounded them. The sound of clanging bones was deafening. The trio was in the thick of a battle they never expected. Brett had two hearts left as he dodged an arrow flying at him. The three grabbed their diamond swords and leaped at the skeletons surrounding them. Brett struck a skeleton, but as he lunged at the bony beast, another arrow struck him. With only one heart left, he tried to battle the skeleton that stood inches from him, but another arrow pierced his arm. The last thing he remembered was Poppy screaming his name.

Brett awoke in his bed to the sound of his front door being ripped from its hinges. He put on armor, picked up his diamond sword, and tore from his bed, but when he reached the living room, three zombies crowded his small doorway. He tried to hold his breath, but the fetid stench was overpowering, and he started to gag. He knew he had to destroy the zombies fast. Brett tried not to breathe as he pulled a bottle of potion from his inventory and splashed it on the undead beasts. The potion weakened them as he sliced into their oozing flesh with his sword. The first hit destroyed the zombie that stood closest to him, but the other two zombies were stronger, and he used all of his energy to rip into the beasts until they dropped rotten flesh on his living room floor.

"Brett!" He heard Poppy's familiar voice in the distance. "Brett!" she called again.

Brett rushed toward the sound of Poppy's voice, but every time he felt he was close by, the voice seemed farther away.

"Poppy!" Brett called out.

"Help!" a faint voice, which sounded like Poppy, cried out in the distance.

"Where are you?" asked Brett, but there was no reply.

Brett pulled a potion of night vision from his inventory and took a sip, enabling him to see in the dark for three minutes. He wanted to use each minute to search for Poppy in the darkness, and after one minute, he was beginning to lose hope. He called her name, but there was still no response.

"Poppy!" Brett screamed, but again, he was met with silence.

He spent the next minute sprinting around Meadow Mews. As he reached Poppy's house, another arrow struck his shoulder. Brett turned around and saw a spider jockey standing inches from him. The skeleton sitting atop the spider shot another arrow at his other shoulder. The arrow grazed his shoulder but didn't break through the skin.

Brett didn't want to spend the next minute battling a hostile mob. He wanted to spend it looking for his friend. This was the last bottle of potion of night vision left in his inventory, and he knew when this potion wore off, it would be almost impossible to find Poppy. He had to battle this tricky hostile mob in seconds, which was another impossibility.

Brett traded in his diamond sword for a bow and arrow and took shelter behind a large oak tree as he shot a barrage of arrows at the skeleton. It took six arrows to knock the skeleton off the spider. Brett pulled out his diamond sword and lunged toward the spider. He slammed his sword into the red-eyed spider, and after delivering a fatal blow, he picked up the spider eye and bone from the ground. With seconds left before the potion wore off, he called for Poppy, but he still heard nothing.

As the potion faded, he heard a rustling in the leaves. "Poppy?" he called out again.

"Brett," a deep voice replied.

"Joe?" Brett called out in the darkness.

"Yes," Joe breathlessly replied.

"Where are you?"

Joe said, "I'm almost at Poppy's house."

Brett didn't need daylight to find Poppy's house. He had traveled there so many times before. He sprinted toward Poppy's front door, but as he reached the house, a loud noise shook the ground.

Kaboom!

"Poppy!" Brett screamed as he watched Poppy's house explode.

"I'm right here." Poppy raced toward the house.

"What happened?" asked Brett as he stood in front of her house staring at the burned remnants of her bungalow.

"I have no idea." Poppy's eyes were filled with tears. "Where's Sam?" she questioned.

"We will find her," Brett promised Poppy, although he knew this wasn't a fair promise. He had no control over what had happened to the ocelot, and he wasn't sure they'd find the animal.

Poppy pulled a torch from her inventory as she sprinted into her house searching for her pet. Smoke filled the living room, and Brett followed closely behind Poppy. His eyes stung from the smoke.

Joe called out from the doorway, "Poppy, I can't believe someone did this to your house. What can I do to help?"

Poppy assessed the damage. "It's not too bad." She looked around the living room. "It looks worse than it is. If I fix the damaged wall, the house should be fine. But I need to find Sam. That's more important than repairing the hole in the wall. Can you help me find her?"

Brett stared at the gaping hole in Poppy's wall and wondered if Sam might have escaped through the hole during the explosion. Before he expressed this idea, the gang heard a meow coming from Poppy's bedroom.

. "I found her!" she called out.

"Now we have to find out who was behind this explosion," said Brett.

"Do you think it was someone who was upset that you play so many practical jokes in Meadow Mews?" suggested Joe.

Poppy dismissed this idea. "We only play jokes on our friends. I don't think any of them would intentionally place a few bricks of TNT near my living room and ignite them."

"Then who do you think did this?" Joe asked.

"I have no idea," Poppy said.

"Do you think it's someone who is jealous you were asked to create that skyscraper in the desert? You mentioned there were a lot of candidates for the job. Maybe someone was upset that you got it," Brett theorized.

"I wonder," Poppy stared at the hole in the wall as she spoke, "but I don't think we have the time to play detective. The truth will come out sooner or later, but we can't be the ones to find out who it is. You have a farm to build, and I have to get ready to TP to the desert."

The sun began to rise. Joe looked up at the sun. "Wow, I spent my first night in Meadow Mews, and it was a lot more intense than I imagined," Joe laughed.

"It's never boring when you hang out with us." Poppy smiled.

"I know we didn't get to sleep," said Brett, "but we have to get to the farm. We have a lot of work we have to do with the irrigation system."

Poppy said, "I have to stay here and repair this wall and head to the desert to build the skyscraper."

"Do you need help repairing the wall?" asked Brett.

"No, it's a simple job, and I have the supplies in my inventory. I appreciate the offer, but it's easier for me to do it alone."

"Okay," said Brett, "but if you need us, let us know."

Poppy paused and then asked, "While I'm gone, if you guys hear anything about the explosion, would you let me know?"

"Of course," Brett replied.

Joe said, "Since I'll be staying here, I will be able to keep a close eye on the house."

"Great," Poppy said. "I can't wait to come back to Meadow Mews and see your completed farm."

"Me too," said Brett. "I can't wait until it's done."

Brett and Joe said their goodbyes to Poppy, but as they walked toward the farm, Brett felt as if someone was watching them. When he mentioned this to Joe, they stopped to see if anyone was trailing them, but there was not a soul around.

4

DOWN THE HOLE

Brett slammed his pickaxe into the grassy, blocky ground, and blue water streamed into the large crater. He said, "It appears that we won't have to create a complicated irrigation system. We have water."

"This is going to be easier than we imagined— that's great. But can you still teach me about irrigation systems?" Joe asked.

"Yes," Brett said as he banged his pickaxe into the ground. "But after we finish this farm," he said as more water filled the blocky hole. He placed dirt over the water.

"Should I put seeds in the ground?" Joe asked.

"Yes," Brett replied. "You're already thinking about the next step. This is a good sign that you'll be a talented farmer."

"Thanks." Joe blushed. He didn't react well to compliments. Joe had always dreamed about being a farmer as a kid, and he was glad this was becoming a reality. However, he wanted to please Brett and make sure he was the best student. This fear of failure was also making Joe a bit insecure. He constantly second-guessed himself and asked Brett about every step in the process. Joe pulled seeds from his inventory and buried them in the ground as two sheep roamed past them in the pasture.

"Are these the right seeds?" asked Joe.

Brett walked over and inspected the seeds. "Yes, these are the right ones." He paused. "You seem to know a lot about farming."

"I just don't want to do anything wrong," confessed Joe.

"That's how we learn," Brett explained. "You should have seen all of the messes I made when I was learning how to farm. I built one irrigation system about twenty times before I got it right."

"Twenty times?" Joe couldn't believe that Brett ever had any issues crafting a farm.

"That's how you learn. Even if you have a talent, you still have to work extremely hard to get better at it," said Brett.

Joe placed seeds in the ground until there weren't any left in his inventory. "Do you have any seeds, or should I gather some more?"

"I have seeds." Brett pulled seeds from his inventory and placed them in the ground. "I think we're going to finish this farm ahead of schedule."

"Wow," Joe exclaimed. "I'm excited to see it finished."

Brett placed the final seed in the ground and asked, "Can you get me some more seeds? There's some tall grass over there." Brett pointed toward the pasture with the sheep. "Just break the grass and get the seeds."

"Of course," Joe replied as he walked toward the pasture.

Not long after, Brett heard his friend scream for help.

"Joe! Are you okay?" Brett hollered as he ran toward him. Brett realized that he had never filled in the hole that he had dug with Poppy, and Joe must have fallen into it. Brett raced toward the hole and looked for Joe, but he was missing. There was no response. Brett was confused. The hole he had dug with Poppy was shallow.

"Joe?" Brett called out, "Where did you go?"

Again, there was silence. "Joe?" Brett called out again, but still he heard nothing. Brett leaned down to inspect the hole, but he slipped on the dirt and fell into it. As he fell farther down the hole, he felt a strong wind of frigid air. This bitter, cold wind blew his blond hair into his eyes and gave him goose bumps. He was freezing, and the sweat on his forehead was turning into a thin layer of ice. He tried to call out for help, but he couldn't hear his own voice over the sound of wind blowing in circles through the narrow hole. His blue T-shirt wasn't enough to keep him warm. He was shivering. Brett looked down, but it seemed like he would never stop falling. He had never had an experience in his life that was similar to this one. The closest was when he was on a portal to the Nether or the End, but this was different because he wasn't surrounded in mist.

Brett screamed "Help!" He still couldn't hear his own voice. The wind grew stronger, and Brett feared he'd freeze to death. He couldn't feel his toes as he fell deeper into the seemingly never-ending hole in the ground. It felt like hours before he landed. When he did, he fell onto the dirt ground with a thump. He tried to stand up, but he felt as if he might fall over. Luckily, he landed by a large oak tree and was able to steady himself with the tree's trunk. He stared at the sun through the leaves in the tree. He had to move away from the shade and get into the sun to warm up. When he gathered enough energy and stability, he did just that. The sun felt good on his skin. The ice on his forehead began to melt.

When he began to feel better, he realized he was alone. He called out, "Hello! Anybody there?" but he was met with silence. Brett grabbed a bottle of milk from his inventory and took a sip. His energy levels were restored, and he gathered the strength and courage to walk around the grassy field. The area looked familiar and unfamiliar at the same time. It reminded him of Meadow Mews, but he wasn't sure why.

Brett tried to find a village. He hoped that he'd meet someone who might be familiar with his town and could give him directions home. Or perhaps he'd encounter someone who had a map or could help him craft one. He walked toward the small village, which looked similar to the one in Meadow Mews. Like his town, the first shop upon entering the village was the blacksmith. Brett walked inside and saw a familiar face behind the counter.

"Lou?" asked Brett.

Brett was so pleased that he was still in Meadow Mews. He couldn't believe it. Despite being home, there was something a bit unfamiliar about the town.

"Yes," Lou the Blacksmith responded. "Who are you?"

"I'm Brett," he replied. "Why don't you recognize me? We've known each other for years."

"We have?" Lou was shocked. "I've never seen you before in my life."

"Lou," Brett said, "I just came in yesterday and traded some wheat for emeralds. You told me about how much you love the apples I grow on my farm and how pleased you were that I'm building a large farm for Meadow Mews."

"What? Meadow Mews is getting a new farm?" questioned Lou.

"Yes," Brett explained. "I have an apprentice named Joe."

"I haven't heard anything about it," Lou said.

"But Poppy and I were telling you about it the other day," said Brett.

"Poppy?"

Brett excused himself and walked outside. He looked for Poppy's signature building, which stood right outside of Meadow Mews village. It was a large castle and people traveled from across the Overworld to tour it. It was missing.

5

WHERE ARE WE?

Brett wasn't sure what had happened. There were so many signs that he was in Meadow Mews, but so much had changed. He hurried toward the spot where Poppy had built the castle. He hoped he'd find some remnants of the great castle. As he reached the patch of grass where the castle had stood, he found nothing. The grass looked as if it had never been touched.

"Brett!" a voice called out.

Brett was shocked to hear someone call his name. He turned around to see Joe approaching him. He was relieved when he saw Joe.

"Brett?" Joe asked. "Where are we? What happened?"

Brett looked around. "I think we're in Meadow Mews, but I'm not sure. Truthfully, I have no idea where we are."

"Me neither," said Joe. "And why do you think this is Meadow Mews?"

"Good question," said Brett as he pulled some more milk from his inventory. He took a sip and handed the bottle to Joe, offering it to him. "When I went to the blacksmith shop, I met the same blacksmith who works in the shop in Meadow Mews. His name is Lou, and I thought I was pretty good friends with him, but when I spoke to him, he had no idea who I was."

Joe sipped the milk. "That's strange."

"I agree," Brett said.

Joe handed the milk back to Brett. "Should we explore the area?"

Brett looked up at the sky. The sun was shining, and it didn't show any signs of setting. "Yes, we should, and we should also try to build some kind of shelter. I have a feeling that my house isn't going to be here."

"Well, we should check out if it's still standing. Maybe when we fell down the hole, something also happened to Meadow Mews. Perhaps everyone lost their memories?"

"But what's really strange is Poppy's castle isn't outside of town." Brett pointed to the spot where the grand castle usually stood.

"That is odd. I love that castle. It was the first place I visited when I came to Meadow Mews." Joe wondered, "Do you think somebody knocked it down?"

"No," replied Brett. "There's no sign that the castle was ever there. I looked at the grass, and it looked as if nobody had ever built anything on it."

Joe theorized, "I know this is going to sound really crazy, but do you think that hole in the ground was actually a portal to the past? Like we're here before all of the places were built? Before you and Poppy were born?"

"It sounds a little far-fetched. I mean, people can't travel through time," said Brett.

"I read a book about a kid who traveled in a time machine," said Joe.

"Yeah, stuff like that happens in books, but not in real life." Brett was annoyed. He looked up at the sky, and the sun was beginning to set. "I'm exhausted. Let's see if my house is still around, and if it is, we can stay there."

"And if it isn't?"

Brett sighed. "We'll have to build a new one."

The duo walked through the familiar roadways of Meadow Mews, but as Brett passed a few homes he recognized, many of the homes were missing. Brett pointed at an empty patch of land. "That's where my friend Roland lives. His house is missing too."

"I'm telling you," said Joe, "we have traveled back to the past."

"If that's true," Brett asked, "how are we going to get back to the time where we were living?"

"I don't know," Joe replied, "but we're going to have to figure it out."

The sky grew darker, and the duo worried they would be attacked by hostile mobs. They talked about what they should do to prepare. As they spoke, Brett recognized a person in the distance. "That's my neighbor George," he said. "I have to stop him and ask him what is happening."

Brett sprinted to George and called out his name. George turned around. "Hi. Who are you?"

"George, don't you remember me?" Brett asked. "I'm your neighbor. I've lived down the road from you for years."

"You do?" George stared at Brett, but he didn't recognize him.

"I brought you wheat the other day. You were there when the mayor announced the opening of the new farm," Brett blurted out.

"Listen," George said, "I'm sorry, but I have no idea what you're talking about, and it's getting late. I must go home."

"Really? You've never seen me before?" Tears filled Brett's eyes. "What is going on? Why doesn't anybody remember me?"

"I'm sorry. I wish I did," said George, and he dashed toward his house.

Joe asked, "What are we going to do?"

"We have to find a place to stay," said Brett. "It doesn't appear that George would let us stay with him."

"Maybe your house is there," suggested Joe.

The duo hurried toward Brett's house, but it was also missing. Brett said, "I knew it wouldn't be here." He looked across the road for Poppy's house, but that was also missing. "Poppy's house is gone too."

Evening turned to nighttime, and they heard the sound of clanging bones in the distance.

"Oh no," cried Joe. "We're going to have to battle skeletons."

"Shhh!" warned Brett. "We don't want them to find us." He quickly grabbed a wooden plank from his inventory and tried to craft a house.

Joe pulled out a torch to give them light as they built a house in record time. When the structure was completed, Brett remarked, "I wish Poppy could see us. She'd be so impressed."

They placed the torch by the front door and walked into the house. While crafting beds, they heard a rumbling at the door.

"Who could that be?" Joe stared at the door.

Brett took a deep breath. "I know that smell."

Joe's nostrils caught a whiff of the fetid odor emanating underneath the doorway. "Zombies," he cried as he pulled his diamond armor and a sword from his inventory. Brett did the same. Then they opened the door before it could be ripped from its hinges and raced outside to battle the zombies that wanted to feast on their flesh.

6

OLD NEIGHBORS

"Six zombies!" Joe shouted.

"Oh no!" Brett plunged his sword into the zombie blocking the doorway. Joe bolted past him to attack the zombies on the side of the house.

Brett was face-to-face with the lone zombie. He took a deep breath as he destroyed the smelly undead beast with three hits, but he wasn't able to pick up the rotten flesh that dropped to the ground because another zombie leaped at him. The zombie grabbed Brett's arm, and he lost a heart. He yanked his arm away from the zombie, enabling him to strike the beast and destroy it. As he struck another zombie lumbering toward him, he could hear a commotion in the distance that sounded like other people battling zombies.

"Joe," he called out, "do you hear that noise?"

Joe could barely answer Brett. "Yes. It sounds as if people are battling zombies in the field."

"We have to destroy these zombies so we can help them," Brett shouted as he sliced into another zombie, destroying the undead monster.

Joe was exhausted. He let out a sigh as he slammed his sword into a zombie, but it didn't make an impact. The zombie had incredible strength. He didn't feel like they'd ever be able to destroy the zombies and help someone else. "Okay, if we survive," he said faintly.

Brett destroyed another vacant-eyed zombie with his diamond sword and then rushed to Joe to help him defeat the three zombies that were destroying Joe's health bar. Brett splashed potions on the zombies and then struck the undead beasts with his diamond sword. Joe only had one heart left. Brett noticed Joe's weakened state and called out, "Take some milk or a potion of healing. I'll take care of these beasts."

Joe sipped the potion as he watched his friend destroy the remaining zombies. When his health bar was restored, he commended Brett, "You're a very strong fighter."

"Thanks, but I don't enjoy it. I'd rather spend my days on the farm," said Joe modestly.

"Well, your talent is coming in handy now," Brett said as he pointed in the direction of the voices. They were growing louder.

The duo sprinted toward the voices when Joe cried out in pain.

"Are you okay?" asked Brett.

"My shoulder," Joe hollered. "It hurts so much."

Brett stopped to grab a bottle of milk to give Joe,

then his own shoulder began to sting. He turned around. "Oh no," he shouted. Three skeletons stood behind them.

Joe fearlessly charged toward the skeletons, destroying one with two blows from his sword. Brett grabbed two bottles of potion from his inventory and splashed them on the bony beasts. The skeletons were weakened but still ready to battle. The duo destroyed the skeletons and ran to join the battle in the distance.

It was dark, and Brett couldn't see. He tripped over a tree trunk and landed on his face. Joe helped him up and then pulled a bottle from his inventory. "Drink this," he instructed Brett.

"What is it?"

Joe replied, "A potion for night vision. It will help you."

Brett took a sip, and his vision improved. He could see the people in the distance and noticed two of his neighbors. Brett called out, "Helen! Franklin!"

The two neighbors had just slain a group of zombies and turned around to see who was calling out their names.

Brett ran toward them. "I'm so glad to see you guys. This is crazy. Why are we being attacked? I mean, what's going to happen next? Are we going to see a chicken jockey?"

"A chicken jockey? What's that?" asked Helen.

"Who are you?" Franklin questioned as he stared at Brett.

"Me?" Brett was annoyed. He wasn't sure why

everyone in town had forgotten him. "I'm your neighbor. Brett. I'm a farmer," he clarified. "Franklin, I gave you apples yesterday, remember?"

"Apples?" Franklin looked confused. "From where? Our town doesn't have a farm."

"What?" Brett began to protest, but then he paused and looked in the direction of the town farm. The potion was still working, and his vision was excellent, but he didn't see the farm. "What happened to the farm?"

"I don't know what you're talking about," Helen said.

"And we have no idea who you are," added Franklin.

As Brett's potion wore off, the sun began to rise. He stared in the direction of the farm and looked at Joe. "Maybe you're right. Maybe we did go back in time."

Joe questioned Franklin and Helen, "Are you sure you've never seen my friend Brett?"

"No," they said in unison.

Joe asked them, "Has there ever been a large castle right outside of the town's village?"

"A castle?" asked Franklin. "What are you talking about?"

"Who is the mayor of the town?" asked Brett.

Helen laughed. "Our town doesn't have a mayor. We just formed Meadow Mews a few months ago."

Brett looked at Joe. "We went back in time."

Franklin smiled and questioned with a giggle. "You guys are time travelers?"

"Guess so," said Brett.

"It wasn't intentional," added Joe.

Helen adjusted her long red hair. "Do I look the same in the future?"

"Yes," Brett confirmed, "you only made one change to your skin. You wear a blue T-shirt now, not a red one."

"A blue T-shirt." Helen looked down at her red shirt. "That might be nicer than this old T-shirt." She pointed to a hole in the shirt.

Joe asked, "When we mentioned a chicken jockey before, you guys didn't seem to know what it was."

Franklin said, "And we still don't. What is it?"

Brett explained, "It's a baby zombie riding a chicken."

"Wow!" exclaimed Franklin. "That sounds intense."

"It is," Joe sighed.

"It's really cool," added Brett.

Helen wasn't interested in learning about chicken jockeys. She wanted to hear about the changes to Meadow Mews and how things were in the future. "Is the blacksmith still there? Are there lots of new homes?" She had a long list of questions.

"Yes." Brett surveyed the area. "There are lots of homes here. The town is quite large." As he spoke, his eyes swelled with tears. "It's odd to be in the same place but miss it so much. I want to go home. I miss my friends, and I want to see Poppy."

Joe said, "You have to excuse my friend. He is very upset. This has been an emotional journey for us. You see, we were in the middle of building a farm when we suddenly fell down a hole and wound up in the past."

"I think it wasn't a hole. It was a portal," Brett said as he wiped the tears from his eyes.

"That is so strange," remarked Franklin.

"Do you think you can help us get back home?" Brett looked at them. "Helen, in the future, you're the one everyone goes to when they have a problem. You're known as the ultimate problem-solver."

"Really?" Helen blushed.

"Yes," Brett said, "you always know what to do."

"Maybe I have to grow older to become wise, because truthfully I haven't a clue what we should do."

Franklin suggested, "Maybe we should go back to the spot where you were building the farm. Perhaps the portal is still open?"

"Good idea," said Brett.

Joe looked around. "I was only in Meadow Mews for a little while, so I'm not sure where to go."

Brett said, "I'll lead the way."

This was the first time he was hopeful that they were going to find their way back home.

7

WATCH OUT FOR WITHERS

The sun blazed, and Brett panted as he charged toward the patch of land where they were constructing the farm. When he reached the spot, he carefully inspected the grass, but he couldn't find a hole in the ground.

"Do you guys see anything?" Brett asked.

Joe looked down. "No, I don't."

"Me neither," added Franklin.

"What are we going to do?" cried Brett. "*I want to get back home!*"

"Calm down," Helen soothed Brett. "Screaming and getting upset isn't going to help at all. We will find a way to get you back to Meadow Mews, or at least the Meadow Mews that you know."

Brett took a deep breath and let out a loud sigh. "You're right. There's no point in getting upset. I know we will find our way back home."

Franklin suggested they go back to his house and think of a plan. "We can have breakfast and try to come up with strategies to get you guys back to your home." As they walked to Franklin's house, he rattled off a series of questions about his future. "Do I still build? Do I have more friends? Do I finally construct the large house I always dreamed about?"

"I'm not sure it's a good idea for me to answer any of those questions," Brett replied.

"Why?" Franklin questioned.

"I think you'll be happy with your future. I don't want to tell you anything that might change it. I think you'll be happy with how it turns out."

Franklin was irritated. "That's so vague. Can't you give me just one hint? Let me know what's going to happen?"

Helen said, "Well, they already told us that we will be attacked by chicken jockeys. I'm not looking forward to that happening."

"I regret telling you about that," said Joe. "It was an accident."

Brett was a history buff and had memorized all sorts of facts about Meadow Mews, but he knew he shouldn't share any of those facts with the people from the past. He didn't want to hurt the future of the town. In order to return to the world he knew, he couldn't disrupt the world he was accidentally visiting. Although Brett was upset that he was trapped in the past, he was also excited to watch history occur. He wondered if any major events were about to unfold. He had heard about the Clash of the Withers, which was a monumental part of the town's history as well as the history of the Overworld.

"Have you ever seen a Wither?" asked Brett. He hoped this question was innocent enough and he'd just hear their response, which would help him figure out what time period he and Joe had landed in.

"No," Franklin replied. "I heard they are very dangerous.

"Aren't they those scary beasts that fly through the sky and shoot wither skulls out of three mouths?" asked Helen.

"Yes," replied Brett.

"Well, thankfully, I've never seen one," said Helen.

"Why do you ask?" questioned Franklin.

"No reason. I just wondered what you've encountered in the Overworld. Since I come from the future, I was curious to know what life was like in the past. Can you tell me about your lives? Maybe as I hear you talk, I'll remember some facts from my Minecraft history class. I was a very good student in history class. I've read a lot about the subject," explained Brett.

Helen told Brett and Joe about her journey to Meadow Mews. "As I said before, this is a new town. We just built our houses here a few months ago."

Brett remembered the first chapter in his history book about Meadow Mews. It talked about the founders. He didn't realize that his neighbors Helen and Franklin were a part of the original founders. He had read about Grant, the person who founded Meadow Mews. He asked, "Do you guys know Grant?"

"Yes," said Helen. "He's a good friend of mine. Do you know him in the future?"

Brett didn't want to answer this question. He didn't know Grant. Apparently Grant was never seen after the Clash of the Withers. "I'd love to see Grant," he said and was glad when she didn't ask him anything else.

When they reached Franklin's house, they spotted Grant standing outside his home. "Hello," Grant greeted Brett and Joe. "I haven't met you both."

Helen said, "This is Grant, the founder of Meadow Mews." She pointed at Grant and then Joe and Brett. "And these are my new friends, Joe and Brett."

"I hope you don't mind," said Brett. "We just built a house in your town."

"Why would I mind? The more, the merrier. We want people to settle in the town. This is a free space. Feel free to build a bigger structure if you'd like and also invite friends to move here."

Just hearing the word *friends* made Brett's eyes fill with tears, but he took a deep breath and tried to remain calm. He didn't want Grant knowing that he was from the future. It was hard enough explaining it to Helen and Franklin; he didn't want to tell everyone his story. It was too complicated.

Franklin said, "We were just about to go inside my house and have breakfast. Would you like to join us?"

Grant politely said no and explained that he had to help construct an irrigation system. Brett had to stop himself from volunteering to help, because he knew that one bad move might impact the future of Meadow Mews.

Franklin's living room was cozy. He had an intricate emerald design on his wall. Brett studied all the details. Franklin lived in a large brick house by the water. Although Brett wasn't there when Franklin built the house, he knew it took Franklin a long time to construct. Franklin was one of the most influential builders in the Minecraft universe. He was Poppy's teacher. Brett wanted to talk to Franklin about Poppy and how one day he'd meet his best student and she'd wind up teaching Franklin about the future of building, but instead he kept quiet and looked around Franklin's old home.

Franklin took out a plate of cookies. "I hope you like cookies for breakfast."

"Yes," Joe said as he took a cookie. He hadn't realized how hungry he was until he started eating.

"Thank you," Brett said and then finished the cookie in one bite.

As they ate cookies, Joe and Brett talked about how they would build a new, larger home. Helen reminded them, "Don't you guys want to go back home?"

"Yes," replied Brett and Joe.

"Then we have to come up with ways to get you back there. Since I'm known for my problem-solving abilities, I want to help you solve the problem."

"Do you have any ideas?" asked Joe.

"Can you describe any strange activities that happened that day?" asked Helen.

"I'm not sure what you mean," said Brett.

"Was the sun setting? Did you see a hostile mob? Do you remember anything that was different than the other days that you worked on the farm?" Helen asked them.

Joe said, "This was the first day we had started working on the farm."

"I had been there a few times before," said Brett, "but I really didn't notice anything unusual. We did find a lot of water quite easily, and we thought we'd be ahead of schedule."

"Maybe the water has something to do with the portal," said Helen.

Brett and Joe weren't sure the water and falling down the portal had anything to do with each other, but they didn't have time to explore this option because a loud noise shook the house.

The gang tumbled from the house as the sky turned purple and a three-headed black creature flew around and grew in size.

"What's that?" cried Franklin.

"It's a Wither!" shouted Brett.

"Look!" Helen pointed at the sky. "It's getting bigger. What are we supposed to do?"

"Put on armor," instructed Brett, "and get out your bows and arrows."

Joe fumbled with his armor as he spotted another smaller Wither growing in the sky. "There are two Withers."

"No," Franklin said as he clutched his bow and arrow, "there are three!"

"Oh no." Brett took a deep breath and pulled out his bow and arrow. "It's the rise of the Withers."

"What?" asked Helen.

"Nothing. It's nothing," Brett said. "We just have to fight, and we have to do it now," he ordered as wither skulls flew toward the group.

"Tell me, Brett. Is this the start of something big?" Helen demanded.

"There's no time to talk. We have to battle," Brett said. He fearlessly hurtled toward the Withers and shot arrows at the three beasts that flew above them.

8

LIVING HISTORY

"Watch out!" Brett warned Joe as a skull exploded by his feet.

Joe jumped back and aimed his arrow at the Wither, hitting the beast in the center of its dark chest. The beast lost a heart and was infuriated. The Wither flew toward Joe, and he gathered the courage to stand there and shoot another arrow into the flying menace. The Wither shot a succession of skulls at him. Two exploded by his legs, but they didn't affect his health bar. The Wither flew directly at Joe. He pulled a potion from his inventory and splashed the Wither, but it made the Wither stronger.

"Potions of harming heal the Wither," cried Brett so he pulled a potion of healing and doused a beast that flew too close to them. The Wither lost the heart it had gained and was even more infuriated.

"We're making the Wither angry," warned Brett.

"We have to destroy this beast," Joe said breathlessly. He pulled out a second bottle of potion. He splashed the beast and then quickly shot a barrage of arrows at the Wither, leaving this powerful mob boss with only one heart.

Franklin delivered the final blow to the Wither, striking the beast with his diamond sword as it hovered above the grass. The Wither exploded and dropped a Nether star, which Franklin picked up from the ground.

"I don't deserve this," he said, and he tried to hand the star to Joe.

Joe was busy battling the other Wither, but replied, "Keep it. Looks like we'll all be able to keep a Nether star. Remember, we're in this together."

Helen called out, "There's another one spawning."

Brett sighed. They couldn't keep up with the battle. If new Withers kept spawning, the gang would have no time to recharge their energy, and they definitely wouldn't have time to help him get back home. As he shot an arrow at the Wither that flew toward them, he realized that he was a part of history. When he was in school, he'd read stories about the soldiers and warriors of this famed Wither battle. At that time, he could only imagine what it was like to be in such an intense battle, and now he was getting to experience it. It wasn't as glamorous as it sounded in books: it was tough and exhausting, and it was also scary. If he remembered correctly, this wasn't a short battle.

As he shot another arrow, he tried to recall specific facts from the battle that could help them win faster.

Surely, if he helped speed up the battle, he wouldn't alter the course of history of the Minecraft universe. Or would he? It didn't matter. The exhaustion of the battle had left his mind blank, and he just shot arrow after arrow at the Wither until it exploded and dropped a Nether star, which he placed in his inventory.

"Good job," Helen called out.

"Thanks, but there are still two more Withers," Brett said as he grabbed some milk from his inventory and took a sip to regain his strength before he battled the remaining Withers.

The two Withers flew through the sky as the gang tried to destroy the three-headed beasts with arrows and potions. When the final Wither was destroyed by Helen's arrow, she let out a sigh of relief.

"That battle is over," she said gleefully.

Brett didn't have the heart to tell her that this was just the beginning. He didn't say anything, and when Joe was about to speak, he cut him off and changed the subject.

"Now that the Withers are destroyed, we should try to find a way to get back home," said Brett.

Helen wasn't paying attention to Brett because she was too focused on the battle they had barely survived. She asked, "How do Withers spawn? Are they natural, like the skeletons when it's dark and raining?"

Joe replied, "Somebody has to spawn them unless you are in the Nether."

"How?" Franklin asked.

"Well, you need to have soul sand and wither

skulls, and once you get those items, it's fairly easy to craft them," explained Joe.

"We have to find out who is spawning the Withers," said Franklin. "I think someone is trying to attack Meadow Mews."

"Maybe it's because we just settled here. Could this land belong to someone else? Are they upset?" Helen theorized.

"Brett and Joe, do you know?" asked Franklin.

"What do you mean?" asked Brett.

"You know the history of Meadow Mews. Was this an important part of history? Was it written about?" Helen asked them.

Brett felt a lump in his throat, and his stomach hurt. He had no idea how he should respond.

Joe replied, "I have to admit that I don't know a lot about history. It's embarrassing, but I can't answer a single question about this part of history. Of course, now I've vowed that when I return home, if we are ever able to get there, that I will take every history book out of the library and study up on the history of Minecraft."

"What about you, Brett?" asked Helen.

Brett looked down at the grass as he spoke. He wasn't a good liar, and anyone who knew him well was instantly able to detect when Brett was fibbing, but luckily nobody here knew him very well, and he could get away with a lie. He wasn't happy about lying to these people, but he knew that if he didn't, he might ruin the future. He said, "I don't either. I don't think we covered that in Minecraft history class. Speaking of getting back home, can we focus on helping us get back there?"

"We will," Helen said firmly, "but this is more important at the moment. Our town was just attacked. If you want to get back home, we have to make sure the place you want to visit in the future still exists."

"I understand," Brett replied, but he really didn't. He just wanted to go home. He didn't want to be a soldier in a war he was never meant to partake in. He was upset. He was tired, and he was trying to rack his brain for at least one fact that could help the people of Meadow Mews of the past.

They reached the small village, and Helen spotted Grant in the distance. She hurried toward him.

"We just battled four Withers." She spoke rapidly, firing off all of the details of their battle with the Withers.

"A Wither?" Grant was shocked. "I didn't see it."

The one fact that Brett remembered was that Grant was never seen after the battle. As they spoke, he decided to keep a close eye on Grant. Although he was remembered as a founder, Brett wasn't quite sure if he was also remembered as a hero.

9

CHICKEN JOCKEY

Brett watched Grant's reaction carefully. Grant seemed interested in hearing the story about the Wither but also didn't seem like he believed it. He asked them, "Are you sure you saw Withers? I just can't imagine why or how they would spawn in our sleepy little town."

"I don't know how you didn't hear the explosions," said Franklin. "It was loud and intense." He pulled the Nether star from his inventory. "And I have this Nether star as a souvenir from the battle."

"Wow." Grant held the Nether star. "I'm impressed that you guys were able to battle that tricky beast."

"Not *one* tricky beast. There were *four*," Helen reminded him.

"You guys are heroes," said Grant. "Thank you for saving Meadow Mews from the Withers."

"We are worried somebody is upset that we settled

the town here and they want to scare us off, and that's why they are spawning Withers."

"Withers have to be spawned?" asked Grant.

"Yes," replied Joe.

"I wasn't sure because I've never been interested in hostile mobs. I just like building towns," explained Grant.

"Have you built other towns?" asked Brett. He didn't recall reading about towns that Grant had founded.

"Yes, I just finished a town by the water called Farmer's Bay. It's very nice. It has a beach, and the residents have built beach bungalows," he explained. "And before that I helped construct a neighboring town, Verdant Valley."

"I'm from Farmer's Bay," said Joe.

"Really? How come we've never met?" asked Grant. Joe didn't reply.

"Wow," said Brett, "you must know a lot about developing towns. When you built those towns, did you encounter any issues with people who lived there before you settled in the town?"

"No," said Grant, "I've never had any issues. I've always worked with people and helped them build homes and communities where they wouldn't have to battle mobs alone. All of the towns I have built are peaceful and have been growing. They are popular places to move to."

"This might be different from the other towns," said Brett. "Perhaps somebody is upset that we are here."

"But who?" asked Grant.

"I don't know," answered Brett, "but we have to find out."

Helen smiled. "I'm going to work with my three friends, Franklin, Joe, and Brett, and we're going to find out who spawned the Withers. Now that the mobs are gone, we have time to investigate."

Brett knew they didn't have that much time. However, he didn't realize how little time they did have. As they spoke, the sky darkened as a beast formed in the sky and blocked the sun.

"No!" Helen cried. "Not another Wither!"

"Look!" Joe yelled. "There is another one spawning."

Grant stuttered, "What d-do we do? I have n-never seen a Wither before."

"Put on some armor," ordered Brett.

"Get out a bow and arrow," Joe instructed.

Brett had already shot a sea of arrows at one of the Withers as it was gaining its strength. This early attack on the Wither helped the gang to defeat that Wither in record time. The Nether star dropped to the floor, and Joe called out, "Brett you earned that one."

The gang marveled as they watched Grant shoot arrows that weakened the second Wither. Alone, he battled the Wither and destroyed the powerful beast in minutes. The Nether star fell to the ground, and he picked it up and held it in his hands.

"Wow." Grant stared at the star. "I never thought I'd be able to defeat a Wither. This is a special star."

Brett watched Grant and realized he had read about

this exact moment in the history books. Grant was in there, but at some point, he disappeared. Brett wondered if he left because he was off to settle a new town, but he wasn't sure. He would have to wait to see what happened to Grant.

All of the villagers were standing in front of their shops. They had watched the battle but were unable to help. Heather the Librarian stood in front of the library. Lou the Blacksmith said, "It's so hard to watch you guys save our town when we can't do anything."

"Don't say that," Grant said. "You guys are very helpful. If it wasn't for you Lou, where would we get armor?" Grant looked at Heather the Librarian. "If it wasn't for Heather, we'd have no access to books. We need those to learn."

"I guess you're right," said Lou.

Helen interrupted, "We should get back to our homes. It's getting dark."

Before they could walk back to their homes, they heard a thunderous boom, and lightning struck, almost hitting the roof of the library.

Skeletons shot arrows at them, and zombies lumbered through the narrow village streets.

The gang was overwhelmed by hostile mobs as they pulled out their diamond swords and attacked the undead beasts that surrounded them. Helen didn't notice a baby zombie riding a chicken.

"What is that?" exclaimed Grant.

"Helen!" Joe warned her, but it was too late. Helen had lost too many hearts in her battle with the skeletons and zombies. The chicken jockey leaped at her, and she was destroyed.

Brett couldn't believe he had just watched the first spawning of a chicken jockey. It was one of the most important moments in Minecraft history, and he saw it with his own eyes. Yet he couldn't get distracted with watching history unfold; he had to help battle the skeletons and zombies while keeping an eye out for chicken jockeys. Joe was able to wipe out the one that had destroyed Helen, with a blow from his sword.

The rain grew harder and soaked the grassy village streets. Grant almost tripped in a puddle, but he steadied himself and began to attack the skeleton that aimed an arrow at him. As he struck the skeleton, he asked Joe, "Have you seen one of those before? Where? I've never heard of them."

Joe said, "I see them all the time where I come from."

"Where are you from?" asked Grant.

"Meadow Mews," he replied, but Grant didn't understand Joe.

"What? No, you're not," Grant said as he plunged his sword into the bony beast and destroyed it. The rain stopped, but the sky was still dark as night approached.

"We have to head back to our homes," said Franklin.

Grant suggested, "Maybe everyone can come to my house. I want to figure out why I didn't know Joe was living in Farmer's Bay and Brett was living in Meadow Mews and how he knows about chicken jockeys."

Joe smiled. "Okay, but it's going to be a long night."

10

PROBLEMS IN THE PAST

"Both of you are from the future?" Grant didn't believe it and challenged them, "Prove it."

"I'm not sure how we can prove it," said Brett.

"Tell me something that will happen soon," said Grant.

"I don't think that's a good idea," Brett replied.

"Me neither," said Joe.

"I just have to trust you?" asked Grant.

"Yes," said Joe.

"We did," Helen said, and she told Grant how they went to the place where Joe and Brett were building a farm in Meadow Mews.

"Was there anything there?" asked Grant.

"No," Helen replied.

"I am going to trust you guys, but can't you see why this story sounds suspicious?" questioned Grant.

"Why would we make something up like this? I mean, what benefit does it have? I just want to go back home." Tears filled Brett's eyes as he spoke. He missed Poppy. He missed his farm. He missed Meadow Mews. He wondered what Mayor Allens and everyone else thought about their disappearance. Were people looking for them? Were they searching throughout the Overworld? He couldn't imagine how worried his friends were because he was missing. He wished he could just go back, but it wasn't that easy.

"I think I can help you get back home," said Grant.

"How?" asked Brett.

"When I was building my house, I noticed a strange hole in the ground. I tried to fill it in with blocks, but it never got full. Perhaps that's a portal back to your time period," suggested Grant.

"Oh my!" Joe stood up and looked around Grant's living room. "Where is it? I need to find it."

Grant walked them to the bedroom. "It's right outside my bedroom window." As they clustered by the window in the small bedroom, they could hear a noise at the door.

"Did you hear that?" asked Helen.

Brett wasn't listening. He was too busy trying to locate the hole from the bedroom window, but he couldn't see the ground. It was too dark out, and the window was too high.

"Help!" Helen screamed from the living room.

"What?" Franklin called out.

"Zombies," she said breathlessly. "We are being invaded by zombies."

Brett dashed into the living room, which reeked of rotten flesh. He readjusted his armor, pulled out his diamond sword and slammed it into the belly of a zombie that stood inches from him. As he struck the beast again, he tried to hold his breath. He was feeling light-headed, but it was better than smelling the putrid smell that permeated the air of Grant's small home.

Grant threw potions on the zombies to weaken them as the gang used their diamond swords to annihilate the walking dead that had broken into the home. When the final zombie was destroyed, Grant put his door back on the hinges and pulled out a torch from his inventory. "It looks like all of the monsters are gone. We can go see that hole if you'd like."

Brett was the first person to bolt out the door toward the hole, but as he reached the spot where Grant had said there was a hole, his heart sunk. It wasn't there.

"Where is it?" Brett asked. He was desperate to get back home, and he tried to hold back the tears and remain calm, but it was virtually impossible.

Grant stood by the window. "That is so odd. There was a hole here this morning. I kept checking on it because I thought it was so strange. I don't know what to tell you, except maybe it will happen again and there will be a hole in the ground."

"So we just have to sit around and wait for that to happen?" Brett's voice cracked as he spoke.

"I think we should go back in to the house," suggested Grant. "It's still dark out, and we're all vulnerable to hostile mobs."

"We should get some sleep," said Helen.

"I have an extra bedroom, so we can all stay here," said Grant.

Joe walked next to Brett as they made their way back inside the house. He said, "It's going to be okay. I just know it. We're going to get back home."

"I wish I could be as hopeful," said Brett. He wished he had never heard about Grant's hole. That had given him hope, and now he was just left hopeless. Walking back inside the house, he crawled into the bed and covered himself with the wool blanket. It was strange to sleep in a bed in a town that he knew so well and yet to be so far away from home. He wished that the hole would resurface as he slept and that once he woke up, he'd be able to jump inside and see all of his old friends. Brett had a hard time sleeping through the night. In the morning, the sun shone through the bedroom window. Brett called out to Joe, but he wasn't in the bed next to him like he had been the night before. He got up from the bed and looked around Grant's home, but it was empty. He was the only one there.

"Joe! Grant! Helen! Franklin!" He called out their names, but he was met with silence.

11

IN THE MIDDLE OF THE NIGHT

Brett hurried out of the house and through the grassy roads of Meadow Mews as he called out everyone's names. His friends were nowhere to be found, and he was worried. He didn't want to be abandoned in the past. He wanted to get back home. Brett sprinted back to the house and to the spot where Grant had said there was a hole. Perhaps they all had fallen down the hole and were in the future while he was still stuck in the past. When he reached the side of the house, he looked down on the ground, searching for any sign of a hole, but there wasn't one.

"Brett," Joe called out.

Brett turned around. "Where were you guys? I was worried!"

"Didn't you hear the Wither?" asked Joe.

Helen ran toward them, panting and trying to catch her breath. "Where were you, Brett?"

"I was sleeping. When I awoke, you were both gone," replied Brett.

"A Wither spawned in the middle of the night. I thought everyone was outside battling the Wither," said Grant.

"No, I'm sorry. I must have slept through it," said Brett.

Grant eyed Brett and asked, "Are you the one who is spawning the Wither?"

"Me?" Brett was shocked at this accusation.

Joe defended his friend. "Are you joking? Why would you think Brett spawned the Wither? He would never do something like that."

"I just found it suspicious that he wasn't battling the Wither with us," explained Grant.

"I woke up, and everyone was gone," Brett said. "I thought you had all gone into the future. I had no idea you were fighting the Wither. I'm sorry I slept through the battle. I am a very heavy sleeper."

"Well, we have to stick together during these battles. Next time a Wither spawns in the middle of the night, we will wake you up," said Grant.

"Thanks," said Brett. "I want to help you guys battle the Wither and win this war."

"We are at war?" asked Grant. "Is that what they say in the history books?"

"This is a significant time in history. But I don't know much about it," said Brett.

Joe added, "I think it was one of those battles that didn't quite have an ending. Like we don't know who was responsible for the battle. It's a mystery."

Helen said, "We discussed this before. It's not wise for us to know what the future holds. We don't want to impact the future."

Grant sighed. "We have to figure out who is behind this. We have no clues."

As they spoke, a Wither flashed in the sky. Grant shot a wave of arrows at the Wither, stopping it before it was able to gain strength. He destroyed the Wither and leaped to pick up the Nether star that dropped on the ground.

Grant explained, "If we can destroy the Wither the minute it spawns, then we have a better chance of surviving."

"Last night was awful," Joe said. "We didn't realize the Wither had spawned until it was powerful enough to destroy us with its explosive wither skulls."

Brett felt bad that he wasn't able to help his friends, and he decided he would make it up to them by helping find out who was behind the attacks. He had a plan. "Grant, are you sure this land was empty when you arrived?"

Grant paused. "Actually, there was one person who lived here when we arrived. His name is Alfred, and he seemed fine with us being here. In fact, he said he was lonely and he enjoyed the company."

"We should meet with Alfred. He might have an idea of who is behind these attacks," suggested Brett.

"Good idea," said Grant.

Brett was happy that this plan pleased Grant, and this made Brett feel a lot better about sleeping through the Wither attack.

The gang jogged toward an old stone house deep in the woods. Large oak trees surrounded the house. Grant walked toward the door and opened it. He called out to Alfred, but there was no answer.

The gang stood outside the door waiting for Grant when another Wither spawned in the sky.

"Oh no!" Franklin hollered as he grabbed his bow and arrows and started to shoot at the beast. But he missed, and the Wither gained its full strength and began to fly toward them, shooting a succession of arrows at the beast.

Two wither skulls flew toward Brett. He tried to sprint from them, but he wasn't fast enough, and the skulls hit his body and he was destroyed. He respawned in the bed and charged back to his friends. When he arrived, he cried out when he saw two more Withers flying next to the Wither that had destroyed him.

He sipped some milk and braced himself for a battle against these flying menaces. As he shot an arrow at one Wither, Brett spotted someone running in the distance. The person had a beard and wore a knit hat. He called out to Grant, "Who is that?"

"Where? What?" Grant was aiming his bow and arrow at the Wither and couldn't turn around to look.

Brett rushed toward this stranger, but two wither skulls landed on him, and he awoke in Grant's house. The Wither might have destroyed him again, but at least he had a clue. He needed to talk to the person fleeing from the battle. Brett jumped out of bed, and with a renewed energy, he went to join his friends in battle.

12

SPONTANEOUS SOLDIERS

"We destroyed the Withers," Joe said proudly. "That's great," said Brett, "I wish I could have helped you guys."

"Are you okay?" asked Joe. "You were destroyed twice."

"I know," Brett sighed. "I wasn't a strong fighter."

"You did a fine job," remarked Helen. "It's very hard to battle the Withers. I feel like we're all exhausted from these constant battles."

"I guess you're right," said Brett. "But I have to tell you guys about something I saw when I was battling the Wither. I spotted a man sprinting in the distance. He had a beard and a knit hat."

"A beard and a knit hat?" Grant's voice cracked.

"Why, do you know anybody who fits that description?" asked Brett.

"Yes," he said. "That sounds like a person I knew a long time ago. We settled Farmer's Bay together and then we had a fight. We never spoke again."

"Oh." Brett nodded his head. "This might be the reason we are in the middle of the Wither battle."

"We have to find him," Grant clarified. "His name is Connor."

Helen called out, "Alfred is back!" She rushed over to Alfred, who was carrying apples.

"Alfred," Grant said, "we were waiting for you."

"For me?" asked Alfred. "Why?"

"We wanted to talk about the Wither attacks," said Grant. "We are trying to figure out who might be behind them."

Alfred offered them apples. Grant took one as Alfred said, "I hope you don't think I'm a suspect."

"Nobody is a suspect. We are just trying to gather some information, so we can come up with a reason for these attacks," explained Grant.

"I had a run-in with a very unusual person when I was out gathering food. As I picked an apple from a tree, I met a man who asked me a series of very peculiar questions," Alfred said.

"What did he look like?" asked Helen.

"What type of questions?" wondered Grant.

"Was he wearing a knit hat?" asked Brett.

Alfred was overwhelmed by all of the questions, but he answered them. "He had a knit hat and a beard. He asked me questions about you," he said and pointed to Grant.

"What type of questions?" Grant was upset.

"He wanted to know where your house was and how long you planned on staying here. He asked me if I liked you."

"What did you say?" questioned Grant.

"Obviously, I said I like you," Alfred said with a smile.

"Did you tell him where I live?"

"No, he wasn't happy that I said I liked you, and he splashed a potion of weakness on me. I stood by the apple tree and couldn't pick another apple. My body felt like I couldn't move. I wanted to ask him why he splashed me. That's when I saw the Wither flash across the sky, and then he ran away. I just waited for the potion to wear off, and then I took a sip of a potion of strength. When I came back here, the Withers were gone."

"He's behind this," said Grant.

"We aren't a hundred percent sure. There might be someone else," said Brett. "We can't jump to conclusions."

"Behind the Wither attacks?" asked Alfred.

"Yes," said Grant. "He must be the one, unless Brett is keeping information from us. Are you, Brett?"

Brett was nervous. Grant was shouting at him, and he didn't like being yelled at. His heart beat rapidly, and he said, "What? I am not keeping anything from you."

"Is he?" Grant questioned Joe.

Joe replied, "I don't know as much as Brett does, but I can still reassure you that this is a great mystery in Minecraft history. We don't know why this battle started, but we do know that it doesn't last forever. We live in a period of peace and abundance."

Alfred was confused. "How do you two know about the future of Minecraft?"

Brett and Joe knew they had to repeat their story. No matter how many times they told the story, every time they spoke about their home, they began to tear up. They missed their lives and their friends. They asked Alfred if he had any ideas how they could get back home, just like they asked everyone else they told their story to.

Alfred apologized. "I have no idea. I've never seen a portal to another period in time."

"I think we have to put our dreams of going back home on hold, and we have to help you guys stop this war," said Brett.

Joe spotted someone running off in the distance. "Is that Connor?"

Grant gasped, "It is!"

The gang was about to sprint toward Connor when the sky filled with Withers. This time, five Withers spawned above them.

Brett joked, "There's one for each of us to battle," but nobody laughed. They prepared to fight, as they had all become soldiers in a war they wanted to end.

13

NETHER RETURN

The Wither flew toward Brett, and he struck the beast with his diamond sword, weakening it. Brett was fearless. He wanted to destroy the Wither as fast as he could so they could track down Connor. He didn't want to spend his time escaping burns from the fiery wither skulls. He wanted to destroy the Wither, and he thought using an enchanted diamond sword would get the job done quickly. He didn't seem to be weakening the beast with arrows. The Wither shot a skull at him. The skull landed on his leg. Already weak from the battle, the wither skull left Brett without any hearts. He spawned back in Grant's house. He was disappointed and was losing confidence in his skills as a warrior.

Brett knew he wasn't a born fighter, but he seemed to be doing a lot worse than his friends. None of them had been destroyed by the Wither except for him. When he returned to the battle, the Withers were gone. They had destroyed the Wither that he expected to defeat.

"I'm sorry I couldn't help you guys beat the Withers again," said Brett.

Grant said, "You did a good job. You weakened the Wither. Once you were destroyed, the beast was easily defeated with one hit from an arrow." He handed Brett the Nether star the Wither had dropped. "Take this. You earned it."

"No, I didn't," said Brett.

"Yes, you did." Grant handed the Nether star to Brett.

"We have to find Connor," said Alfred. "I think he is still in the forest where I picked the apples."

"Yes," said Grant. "We have to track him down. I haven't seen him in years, and I have a lot I must tell him."

The gang headed toward the forest. The path was thick with leaves, and they stuck close together so they wouldn't lose each other. Brett spotted Connor by a large oak tree. Connor was in the midst of building a portal. The gang raced toward him, but it was too late. Connor was surrounded by purple mist and on his way to the Nether.

"Let's jump on the portal!" shouted Grant.

The six of them clustered on the portal, and within seconds they were in the middle of the Nether and confronted by ghasts that flew toward them and shot fireballs at them.

"Use your hand," screamed Brett as he watched Helen fumble with her bow and arrow.

"Seriously?" Helen questioned as she slammed her fist into the fireball, assuming this would destroy her. Instead, the fireball flew back toward the ghast and destroyed the fiery beast.

When the final ghast was destroyed, they started their search for Connor. Alfred pointed to a bridge and climbed up the ladder. Everyone followed him. Once they reached the top, Alfred said, "I feel like from here we can see forever, but I don't see Connor anywhere over here."

"I see a Nether fortress," said Helen.

"I bet he's in there," said Grant. "I know Connor, and he is always on the hunt for treasure. In fact, that's what our falling out was over. It was all about treasure. He stole a bunch of treasure from me."

"That's awful," said Franklin as the gang climbed down the stairs and made their way to the Nether fortress.

"Yes." Grant told them the story about his last meeting with Connor. "We were settling Farmer's Bay. We had just gone mining and found a jungle temple on the way home from our trip. We divided the treasure, and I put mine in a chest in the house I had just built in Farmer's Bay. I woke up, and it was missing. I went to talk to Connor, and he confessed to taking it. He told me he felt he deserved it. He said he was the one who unearthed the treasure, when I said that we did it together. He told me he was sick of doing everything together and he was taking his treasure and leaving. I never saw him again."

"Wow," said Brett. "How long were you friends?"

"A very long time. I didn't expect that at all." His eyes filled with tears, and he said, "I miss him. I really enjoyed building towns with him, but I think people always gave me more credit for the towns. I never knew why, but when we created Farmer's Bay and Verdant Valley, people would always refer to me as the founder, but we were partners. I think this bothered him a lot, and that's why he stole the treasure and left. I want to talk to him about it. I want him to know how I feel. He never gave me that chance. He just stole the treasure and left."

"And now he's attacking your new town with Withers," said Brett. "I don't understand why you want to talk to him."

"I think it's a misunderstanding. He was my best friend, and I know he is a good person," explained Grant.

Brett was shocked at how forgiving Grant was, and thought about how he'd react if someone had stolen from him and then started a war on his new town. He remembered how Grant was written about in the history books. He was a legend known for his bravery and character. Brett was glad that he was getting to meet this person. He tried not to focus on the fact that the history books had no mention of Grant after this Clash of the Withers, and he hoped that he would find out what happened to Grant.

"Is this the first town you created after Farmer's Bay?" asked Joe.

Grant laughed. "I guess I didn't make it in the history books."

Brett said, "Well, we don't read them." Again, this was a fib. Brett knew that Grant was known for founding three towns, and this was the only one he founded without Connor.

"This is the first one I founded on my own. It took a long time for me to get over the fact that my best friend had stolen treasures from me. When I was finally ready to leave Farmer's Bay and Verdant Valley, I traveled as far away as I could and settled this town."

Alfred said, "I was so glad you settled here. I felt like I was the only one who lived in this part of the Overworld, and it was lonely."

They were in front of the Nether fortress and were face-to-face with the blazes that were guarding the fortress. Grant pulled snowballs from his inventory and slammed the icy snow into a blaze, destroying it.

"Where did you get snowballs?" asked Alfred.

"I am full of surprises," Grant joked as he threw another snowball at a blaze.

As Brett's arrow destroyed the final blaze, they could hear a voice in the Nether fortress taunting them, "Come and get me."

"That sounds like Connor," Grant whispered.

The gang clutched their diamond swords as they entered the fortress, ready to attack Connor, but when they entered the fortress, it was empty.

14

WHAT YEAR IS THIS?

"**D**o you see anyone?" asked Joe as they each explored a different section of the Nether fortress.

"No." Brett was confused. They heard voices when they were outside the fortress, but where was Connor?

"I don't see him." Grant stood by a patch of Nether wart when they heard a noise.

"What's that?" Harriet called out.

Boing! Boing! Boing! The sound grew louder.

"Oh no!" Franklin hollered. "Magma cubes!"

Brett clutched his diamond sword. He was annoyed. This wasn't the time to battle magma cubes. Not that there was ever a good time to battle magma cubes, but they had to find Connor. However, there was no escape. The magma cubes bounced into the center of the Nether fortress and attacked them. Brett sliced into one of the magma cubes with his diamond sword. The boxy being broke into smaller cubes, and Joe destroyed the mini cubes with a strike from his sword.

"There are more!" warned Franklin as four magma cubes bounced toward them. The group was exhausted from these constant battles, and it was seen in their actions. Franklin dropped a sword. A magma cube attacked Helen because she stood transfixed by the cube's evil red, orange, and yellow eyes, and she lost a heart. Grant passed around a potion of healing, and everyone in the group took a sip. With renewed energy, they were able to destroy the cubes and pick up the magma cream that had dropped onto the floor of the Nether fortress.

When the final cube was gone, Franklin screamed, "Wither skeletons!"

Brett slammed his sword into the wither skeleton, destroying the undead Nether mob, and a stone sword dropped to the ground. "Oh wow," marveled Brett, "I never got one of these before." He picked up the stone sword and placed it in his inventory.

"Good job. Those are very rare," said Grant.

Helen wasn't paying attention to Brett's rare reward. She stood in the hallway and called out in a hushed whisper, "Guys, I think I hear something. Come here."

"What?" Franklin zipped toward her.

"I hear something," she said. "It sounds like voices."

The gang stood in silence, but they didn't hear any voices. Alfred said, "I don't hear anything, but we should investigate."

Franklin suggested, "No, I think we should find out if someone looted the treasure."

"Treasure hunting now?" Helen was appalled at this idea.

Franklin defended himself. "Restocking our resources is a good idea. When we return to the Overworld, we will have to battle Withers. We are running low on various supplies. This would be an easy way to give us an advantage in battle."

Helen said, "Shhh! Do you hear them?"

The group stood silently again, and they could hear a noise coming from down the hall. With their diamond swords in their hands, they crept down the hall of the Nether fortress, passing up the opportunity to gather treasure. They searched through each room, and when they reached the last room, they saw a chest on the floor and a person in a black knit hat leaning over the opened chest.

"Connor," Grant called out.

The person turned around, but it was a girl with large blue eyes. Brett recognized her.

"Nancy?" he asked.

"Brett?" Nancy questioned.

Nancy was a well-known treasure hunter in Meadow Mews, and Brett was relieved to see her. This meant he was back in his time period.

"You recognize me?" Brett asked.

"Of course," Nancy said. "You live down the block from me. I'm still annoyed that you and Poppy pulled that prank on me. I tried to get back at you guys. I placed a TNT brick by her wall."

"That was you?" Brett was shocked.

"I know. I meant to apologize, but Poppy left before I was able to," she said.

"Do you know me?" asked Joe.

"Yes, I was at the grand opening of the farm. I recognize you, Joe."

"I can't believe it!" Brett said.

Nancy was confused. "Why are you acting so weird? And who are your friends? I hope they don't try to steal my treasure. This is a solo mission, and I was here first."

"No, this is your treasure. You can have it," said Brett. "But can I travel back on the portal to Meadow Mews with you?"

"Of course," she said as she filled her inventory with the gold ingots that she picked up from the chest.

"Great! Joe, we get to go home!" Brett looked over at Joe.

Grant wasn't happy about Brett's decision to abandon them, and he said, "You're done helping us?"

"I'm sorry," said Brett, "this was never a battle that I was supposed to fight."

Joe said, "I know we weren't meant to fight their battle, but we are involved, and we can't just walk away from our friends when they are in trouble."

"Joe," Brett explained, "we have the opportunity to go home and finish the farm. We have to let the people from the past battle their own wars. It's bad enough that we were involved with it at all. We could have altered the course of history."

Nancy placed the final gold ingot in her inventory

and remarked, "I have no idea what you guys are talking about, but if you want to go back to Meadow Mews with me, you should come with me now. I have gathered all of the treasure I need, and I have to get back home."

Joe asked Nancy, "Do people notice that we are missing back home?"

Nancy said, "I have no idea. I left right after the grand opening of the farm. Are you missing? I see you guys here."

"We were, but . . ." Brett said and then stopped. He didn't want to tell Nancy the entire story because he knew he would sound like a deserter.

"But what?" asked Nancy. "I don't have all day. I have to get back to Meadow Mews."

Brett walked behind Nancy, but he turned around when he saw Joe standing next to Grant, Alfred, Helen, and Franklin.

"Joe?" he asked.

"I'm sorry, Brett. I know I'm supposed to be your assistant, but I can't go with you. I have to stay and help them," explained Joe.

"But what happens if we never have another chance to make it back home?" asked Brett.

"That's a risk I'm willing to take," said Joe.

Brett stood and stared at Joe, and Nancy called out again, "Come on Brett. It's now or never!"

Brett was confused and hoped that Nancy's words weren't true.

15

NETHER MEANT TO HURT YOU

"Come on, Brett!" Nancy called out again.

As Brett tried to make his decision, arrows flew through the Nether fortress, landing on Grant's shoulder.

"Grant! Are you okay?" Brett darted to his friend.

Nancy didn't stick around to watch the battle. She didn't even tell Brett she was leaving. When he turned around to see her, she was gone.

Grant held his shoulder. "No, I'm weak. I only have two hearts left. Do you have a potion of healing?"

As Brett looked through his inventory, an arrow landed on his arm. He also only had a couple of hearts left, and when he pulled the potion from his inventory, he realized he only had enough potion for one of them.

"I only have a small bottle," he explained as another arrow landed on his arm. "Let's each take a small sip and see if it helps us."

"It won't work," said Grant as an arrow struck his shoulder, leaving him with one heart.

Brett handed Grant the potion. "You need this more than I do."

Grant sipped the potion and regained his energy. He rushed in the direction of the arrows. He tried to avoid getting shot as he raced toward the person who was attacking them.

As Grant leaped toward their attacker, Joe raced over to Brett. He handed him a potion of healing. "Take this," he said. "You made the right decision. We can't abandon our friends."

"But we may never see our home again," Brett said as he sipped the potion.

"It's a chance we had to take. We are too invested in helping Meadow Mews survive. We can't walk away now," Joe remarked and then bolted toward Grant.

Grant was charging down a hall as arrows flew toward him. One arrow struck his leg when he saw the person who was attacking them.

"Connor! Stop!" Grant screamed.

"Never!" Connor called out.

"Why are you doing this?" asked Grant. "You're the one who stole my treasure! What did I ever do to you?"

Connor didn't say a word. He pulled a potion of harming from his inventory and splashed it on Grant.

Franklin, Helen, and Alfred were hurrying down the hall toward Grant. Brett and Joe followed closely behind.

"You are outnumbered," Grant told Connor. "Let's

end this battle and talk. I don't want to fight with you. We used to be friends."

"That's right, we used to be friends, but we aren't friends anymore. I have nothing to say to you," said Connor.

"I'm sorry for what happened," Grant said.

The gang looked shocked. They wanted to know why Grant was apologizing.

"There are no words that can ever make up what you did to me." Connor aimed his arrow at Grant and shot. The arrow pierced Grant's shoulder and he cried out in pain.

"Stop," Grant pleaded. "I can explain."

"I don't think you can," screamed Connor.

"Please, let him speak." Brett raised his voice as they hastened toward Connor. "Grant is trying to apologize. Listen to him."

"Why?" asked Connor. "You don't know Grant. He is going to hurt you guys."

"What happened between you two?" asked Helen.

Connor looked at Grant and told Helen, "Why don't you ask him?"

Grant stood in silence as everyone stared at him, waiting for his reply. A few minutes passed, and Brett said, "Grant. Can't you tell us what happened?"

He stood silently.

"I told you." Connor laughed. "He is guilty, and he doesn't want to admit it."

"No, I'm not," screamed Grant.

"Then tell them how you abandoned me. They need to know the real story. How you tried to write me out of the history books and claimed that you discovered Farmer's Bay and Verdant Valley on your own."

"I never did that. People just gave me credit. It wasn't my fault," Grant said softly.

"You took all the credit. You told everyone that you were the only one who founded these lands, and when I wanted some credit for cofounding these towns, you tried to get rid of me," said Connor. His voice cracked, and he was very upset. "And now it's payback. I am going to destroy the one town that you actually did create on your own."

Grant said, "You're right. I did do those things. I'm sorry."

"It's too late," Connor screamed. "I am going to destroy Meadow Mews."

Connor doused the group with a potion of weakness and then splashed a potion of invisibility on himself and disappeared.

"We have to find him," said Grant. His voice was weak.

Helen gathered enough energy to pull a potion of healing from her inventory and passed it along to her friends. Instantly they were reenergized and dashed out of the Nether fortress to find Connor.

"We are never going to find him," said Brett. "He is probably back in the Overworld. There is no way he was going to stick around the Nether. He is intent on destroying Meadow Mews."

"It's all my fault," remarked Grant.

"You have to talk to him again," said Helen.

"I don't think he'll ever accept my apology. He's right. I wasn't a good person," said Grant.

"Maybe you weren't a good person back then, but that's not a reason for Connor to act this way. And anyway, it sounds like both of you are at fault, and now he is hurting innocent people by summoning Withers," said Franklin.

"I bet he picked up a lot of soul sand when he was here. He is probably spawning Withers to attack the people of Meadow Mews at this moment," Grant said.

"We will stop him," exclaimed Helen.

"Once we do, you have to talk to him and explain why you did what you did," added Franklin.

"I don't know why I acted that way. It was my ego, I guess," said Grant.

"Then say that," Helen told Grant.

"This is all my fault," said Grant.

"Stop saying that and start doing something." Brett was angry. He wanted Grant to find Connor and stop this battle. He possibly gave up his one chance at getting back home to help Grant, and now he discovered Grant was the reason the battle was taking place in the first place. Brett was annoyed.

"Look over there!" Helen pointed to a person in a knit cap jogging toward a portal.

"Maybe that's Nancy," said Brett.

"We have to find out," Grant hollered as they hurried as fast as they could toward the portal.

16

BACK TO THE BATTLE

"Connor!" Grant shouted.

The person in the knit hat turned around. It was Connor, and he screamed, "I have enough soul sand to create a never-ending supply of Withers. You are in big trouble."

"What do you want from me? How can I get you to stop these attacks?" asked Grant.

Connor laughed as he hopped on the portal and purple mist surrounded him. The gang joined him the portal and emerged in the middle of the Meadow Mews village.

Heather the Librarian was standing outside the library, and Grant asked her, "Did you see a man with a knit hat?"

"No, I haven't seen anybody," she explained.

Brett scanned the area, but he didn't see Connor. He looked up in the sky, and there weren't any Withers.

"At least we got back here before he started to spawn Withers."

"Yes," Grant sighed with relief, "but we have to find Connor. Where could he be?"

Helen spotted someone in the distance. "Is that him?" She bolted toward the forest outside of Meadow Mews.

The gang followed Helen, but it was hard to see her as she raced down a path thick with leaves.

"Helen!" screamed Brett.

"I'm here!" Helen called out, but Brett didn't see her. He was lost in the forest and couldn't find any of his friends.

He could hear rustling leaves and the sound of arrows flying through the air, but he couldn't find anyone. "Where are you guys?"

"Over here!" Joe called out.

"Where?" Brett made his way through the leafy path and finally saw his friends battling Connor.

Connor put his arms up. "I surrender!"

Grant walked toward Connor. "I want to apologize for my behavior. I was young, and I wanted all of the credit for the towns. I didn't want to share the spotlight."

"We were a team," said Connor. "I trusted you."

"I know you did, and I'm sorry," said Grant, "but I can explain."

"Really?" Connor questioned.

"Yes," Grant said. "When we finished with Verdant Valley, people started to congratulate me. It was incredible because I had never gotten that sort of attention before. They assumed I founded the towns on my own and because I loved the attention, I never corrected them."

"I want to be in the history books. I want to be noted as the cofounder of these towns," declared Connor.

"If I make a public statement and also write that you were the cofounder of Farmer's Bay and Verdant Valley, will you leave the people of Meadow Mews alone? They are innocent people, and they don't deserve to get caught up in this battle. This is our fight. We don't need to involve other people."

Connor said, "I will stop the Wither attacks if you make the statement now."

"Yes," said Grant, "and I will see Heather the Librarian and give her a history book where you are mentioned as the cofounder."

Connor smiled. "Great. I want to see you write it and hand it to Heather."

The group was ready to return to town when a thunderous sound shook the town and the skies darkened. Rain poured down on the group, and they tried to stay dry by hiding underneath the leaves.

"Ouch!" Franklin hollered as an arrow struck his arm.

"Skeletons!" Grant pointed at three skeletons that spawned near a large oak tree.

Grant took out his sword, but before he could attack the skeleton, a silent creeper destroyed him. *Kaboom!*

Connor screamed, "Where is Grant? I knew he'd back out of the deal."

Brett tried to reason with him. "He didn't get destroyed on purpose," Brett said as a sea of arrows flew in his direction. One arrow pierced his shoulder, leaving him with one heart.

"I don't believe you," said Connor. "I can't be tricked by Grant again."

"You're not being tricked," Brett said. He could barely get the words out as he struck the bony beast that stood inches from his face.

Joe said, "Connor, I promise you Grant was being sincere."

"You have no idea what type of person Grant is. Don't be fooled by him," Connor said, and he splashed a potion of invisibility on himself and disappeared.

Brett destroyed the skeleton as Franklin raced toward him and asked, "What happened?"

"Connor is going to attack Meadow Mews," Brett said. As he spoke, he saw a Wither spawn over the village.

"It looks like he started his attack," said Franklin.

"We have to stop him," Brett declared.

Helen noticed Brett's low health bar. As she handed him a potion of healing, she said, "You're going to need this." He took a sip. As he drank, he wondered why Grant hadn't returned. If he had respawned, he'd have enough time to TP back to the battle, but he wasn't there. He contemplated if what Connor had said was true. Maybe they shouldn't trust Grant.

17

THE PAST AND THE FUTURE

The gang sprinted into the town. Alfred screamed, "Look at the sky! There are six Withers! How can we defeat six Withers? We're doomed!"

"Don't say that," said Brett. "We can defeat them."

"How?" Alfred asked.

"We just have to try," Brett said as he jumped through puddles toward the Withers.

The rainy skies made the battle with the Withers challenging. As rain and wither skulls fell down on them, the gang worked hard to stay positive and defeat these creatures. Helen focused on defeating one Wither and shot a series of arrows at the belly of the beast. However, the Wither was stronger than she expected, and it wasn't losing hearts.

"Help!" Helen called out, but everybody was in the middle of their own battle against a Wither and they weren't able to help her.

"Where's Grant?" shouted Brett as he struggled to defeat a Wither. He shot an arrow into the Wither, destroying the beast.

As he darted to pick up a Nether star, a voice called out. "I told you he'd abandon you guys. You can't trust him!"

Brett turned around to see Connor standing by the library. He clutched a book. "I had to write my own history book that tells the truth and states that I am the cofounder of Farmer's Bay and Verdant Valley. Sadly, there is also a section about the destruction of Meadow Mews. I'm sorry, but this town wasn't meant to last."

A familiar voice answered, "Yes, it will!" Grant raced into the center of town and battled the Withers that flew above them. "Stop spawning these Withers!" he demanded.

The rain stopped, and the gang was relieved because it was almost impossible to battle the Withers when it was raining. Connor was annoyed that the rain had stopped and that another Wither had been defeated.

"Don't try to look like a good guy," Connor hollered. "We all know you're the bad guy."

As Grant destroyed a Wither, he called out, "Stop spawning Withers!"

"Never!" shouted Connor. "Not until everyone leaves this town because it's so dangerous and they are afraid to stay here because of the Wither attacks."

"That will never happen," said Brett. "I know that people care about this town too much, and they would never abandon it. So stop attacking it, because you're wasting your time."

"How do you know people won't abandon Meadow Mews? What, can you see into the future?" Connor laughed.

"Maybe I can," Brett said as he helped Joe destroy a Wither.

Helen and Franklin destroyed another Wither while Grant and Alfred annihilated the final Wither. When the sky was empty of hostile mobs, Grant walked toward Connor.

Grant asked, "Can I read the book? I want to see your version of history."

"I'm not going to show it to you," said Connor.

Heather the Librarian walked out of the library. Her white robe flowed in the wind. She approached Connor and asked, "Is this book for the library?"

"Yes," he said and handed her the book. "This is a true story about the founders of Farmer's Bay and Verdant Valley."

"Great," she took the book and opened the pages. "I can't wait to read it."

"May I see it?" asked Brett.

"Don't give it to him," ordered Connor.

Heather explained, "You gave this book to the library. This is a public space, and everyone is allowed to read the books that are on our shelves."

"But he can't read it," Connor hollered.

"Please don't scream at me," she said. "As I said before, this is a public library, and you can't tell me who can read this book. You gave us this book."

Brett read aloud from the book as Connor covered

his ears: "Connor was a founder of Farmer's Bay and Verdant Valley. He was the first person to discover the land, but his ex-partner decided to take all of the credit. Due to this fact, Connor was forced to destroy Meadow Mews. The town of Meadow Mews existed for only a brief period of time. It was overrun with Withers, and the residents moved out."

When Brett was finished reading, Connor removed his hands from his ears. He scanned the group to see their reactions, but they were expressionless.

"This book is predicting the future," said Heather. "I can keep it in the library, but I must shelve it with the novels and other works of fiction."

"This isn't fiction!" protested Connor.

"I'm afraid it is," said Brett, although he wasn't sure he was telling the truth. He feared that he'd return back to his time period and Meadow Mews would be gone.

"I don't understand why you're so confident that the town will still exist," said Connor.

"I have faith that these people want to stay here. Look at how hard the residents are fighting and nobody has left," said Brett.

Joe added, "I have never seen a community stick together like this. Your hate can't bring them down. They are here to stay."

Alfred said, "I have to say that I was here before Grant settled Meadow Mews. When he arrived, he visited me and asked if it was okay to build a town here. At first, I was worried that my quiet life would become noisy. However, the more time I spent with Grant, the more I realized he was a sincere person. I knew that he was going to create a town where people had freedom and where I could make new friends. I am not leaving this area. You can spawn five Withers a day, but I won't budge."

Connor didn't expect this reaction. He said, "I want credit for saving this town."

"Saving it?" questioned Joe.

"Yes, I want to be in the history books as the person who saved Meadow Mews."

"But you're the one trying to destroy it," said Grant.

As they spoke, Brett noticed a small hole by the side of the library. Cold air rose from the hole, creating a mist. He walked over to Joe and said in a hushed whisper, "Do you see that?"

Joe's eyes widened. "Yes." He stepped toward the hole, and as he reached for it, he tripped and fell in, and Brett jumped in after him.

The cold air gave Brett goose bumps as he called out to his friend, but there was no response.

"Joe!" Brett hollered again.

Joe didn't respond. Brett hoped that when he landed he'd be in Meadow Mews and it would still exist. He also wondered if anybody had noticed them sneak off and if anyone went to search for them in the hole. Brett took a deep breath as he plunged deeper down the hole, and he waited until his feet touched the ground.

18

FARM LIFE

T*hump!* Joe landed and stood up. He looked down at the grassy ground and recognized the farm. He spotted Joe, who stood by the ditch they had dug. "We still need more seeds," said Joe.

Brett laughed. "Wow, you want to get back to work right now?"

Joe smiled. "Do you want to see your old home?"

"Yes," said Brett. "And I'd love to see Poppy. She must be worried about us."

The duo walked back to Brett's house. They walked through the town, and Brett walked into the blacksmith shop. Lou called out, "Hi, Brett. How's the farm? Do you need anything?"

Brett's eyes filled with tears of joy. "You recognize me?"

"Of course. Why wouldn't I?"

"Long story," said Brett as he stepped out of the store and saw Joe standing by Poppy's castle.

Joe said, "Poppy is away for her work project. I asked the person who gives tours of the castle."

As they walked toward Brett's house, Mayor Allens approached them. "Taking a break already?"

Brett was surprised that Mayor Allens didn't notice they were missing for days. Brett said, "I just wanted to check on my house."

"Why? Is there a problem?" asked Mayor Allens.

Brett didn't know how to respond. Instead he asked, "When was the last time I saw you?"

Mayor Allens laughed. "Me? Are you joking? I saw you a few minutes ago when we ended the celebration for the farm's grand opening. Are you okay?"

"Yes." Brett smiled. "In fact I've never been better. I think we are going to head back to the farm. We found water underneath the blocks, so we believe we will finish it a lot faster than we expected."

"We just need to get more seeds," said Joe.

Mayor Allens pulled a bunch of seeds from his inventory. "Use these."

"Thank you," said Joe as he gathered the seeds from Mayor Allens.

The duo decided to skip the visit to Brett's house, and they hurried back to the farm. However, they made one side trip. Brett led Joe to the library.

Heather saw them enter the library and walked over. "Do you guys need any help?"

"Yes," said Brett, "we'd like all of the books about the Clash of the Withers."

Heather led them to an aisle filled with books

about that period in history. She walked away and then came back carrying a copy of a familiar book. "There is also this book. It's a novel about that time period, if you're interested. It imagines a world where Meadow Mews was destroyed."

"Thanks," said Brett, "but we'd rather stick to just the nonfiction books."

Brett and Joe checked out a stack of books from the library.

"We have a lot of reading to do," said Joe.

"Yes, we'd better work on the farm now so we have time to read these tonight," suggested Brett.

As they left the library, Brett passed a familiar statue that he had always seen but never paid attention to. His entire life, he had walked by the statue and never stopped to read it. It was a small statue of a Wither. The statue was dedicated to the brave and fearless warriors who fought in the great Clash of the Withers. Underneath the statue there was a plaque and a long list of names of the soldiers who had battled the Withers. Brett leaned down and was stunned to see the names *Brett* and *Joe* on the list.

"It really happened." Brett pointed at Joe's name on the list.

"I guess it did," said Joe.

Helen, Alfred, and Franklin were walking through town when they spotted Brett and Joe standing by the Wither statue.

Helen smiled. "Do you see familiar names on there?"

Brett replied, "We do."

"Thanks for helping us out," said Franklin.

Nancy walked past. "Hey, didn't I just see all of you in the Nether?"

Helen laughed. "Yes, we did see you there."

Brett wanted to ask Helen and the others what had happened to Grant and Connor, but he knew he could read about the history of Meadow Mews in the books they had taken out of the library. After they spent their day working on the farm, Brett and Joe dug into their history books.

Brett stayed over at Poppy's house with Joe. As he read and pet Poppy's ocelot Sam, he looked over at Joe and said, "We're in this book."

Joe smiled. "We made history."

Brett added, "And tomorrow we'll continue to make history when we work on the farm that will help sustain Meadow Mews for years to come."

"I'm glad the people of this town didn't give up and that Meadow Mews is still here today," said Joe.

"Me too," said Brett.

Brett stayed up too late reading history books. There was so much to learn. Now that they had gone back in time and were able to experience the town at that monumental part of history, he was even more excited to learn about the history of the Overworld. Perhaps one day, he'd stumble upon another portal and travel to another time period. For now, he was happy just reading about the past in books.

WANT MORE MINECRAFT ADVENTURES?

Read the Unofficial Overworld Adventure series!

Escape from the
Overworld
DANICA DAVIDSON

Attack on the
Overworld
DANICA DAVIDSON

The Rise of
Herobrine
DANICA DAVIDSON

Down into the
Nether
DANICA DAVIDSON

The Armies of
Herobrine
DANICA DAVIDSON

Battle with the
Wither
DANICA DAVIDSON

Available wherever books are sold!

DO YOU LIKE FICTION FOR MINECRAFTERS?

Read the rest of the Unofficial Overworld Heroes Adventure series to find out what happens to Stevie and the Overworld Heroes!

Adventure Against the Endermen
DANICA DAVIDSON

Mysteries of the Overworld
DANICA DAVIDSON

Danger in the Jungle Temple
DANICA DAVIDSON

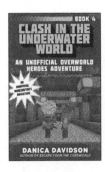

Clash in the Underwater World
DANICA DAVIDSON

The Last of the Ender Crystal
DANICA DAVIDSON

Return of the Ender Dragon
DANICA DAVIDSON

Available wherever books are sold!

DO YOU LIKE FICTION FOR MINECRAFTERS?

Read the
Unofficial Minecrafters Academy series!

Zombie Invasion
WINTER MORGAN

Skeleton Battle
WINTER MORGAN

Battle in the Over-world
WINTER MORGAN

Attack on Minecrafters Academy
WINTER MORGAN

Hidden in the Chest
WINTER MORGAN

Encounters in End City
WINTER MORGAN

Available wherever books are sold!

DO YOU LIKE FICTION FOR MINECRAFTERS?

Read the Unofficial Minecrafters Mysteries Series!

Stolen Treasure
Winter Morgan

Beneath the Blocks
Winter Morgan

The Skeleton Secret
Winter Morgan

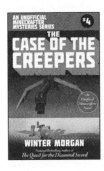

The Case of the Creepers
Winter Morgan

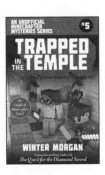

Trapped in the Temple
Winter Morgan

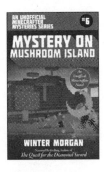

Mystery on Mushroom Island
Winter Morgan